We're the stars!

Usborne Bug Tales

Lola Locust
finds her Focus

Lesley Sims

Illustrated by Siân Roberts

This story is about a bug who finds it hard to focus,

with Harry Hornet,

LOTS of bugs

and lovely
Lola Locust!

Lola's looking for a job.
"I wonder what I'll do?"

She skips along to
Jobs for Bugs.

Harry Hornet hurries up.

Lola isn't listening.

Harry starts to frown.

"You're looking for a job?"
he asks.

"I like to be outside," she says.

Lola's job is at the park.
The gardening bees
buzz, "Hi!"

Lola starts to mow
the grass...

...but stops
to have
a chat.

The sun shines brightly.
Lola sighs.

"What *was* I doing?" Lola thinks. "Something with a tree..."

Snip! Snap!
She cuts the branches off.

"STOP THAT!"
shouts a bee.

15

Lola goes to find a hose.

"STOP THAT!" shout some soggy bugs. "*We didn't want a shower.*"

Lola needs another job.

18

Lola's at the bakery.
She has two jobs to do.

1. Make a cake.
2. Check the bread.

SUGAR

She flings food in the
mixing bowl.

She pours it out, bends down and shouts, "Now, I'll watch it rise!"

The cake is rising
wonderfully...

...but what about
the bread?

Lola turns. "Is something burned?"

The baker nods his head.

They cut a slice
and take a bite.

Please leave!
You cannot bake!

Harry groans.
"You're back again?"

Lola thinks. "I like to drive.
Can I drive a bus?"

"No!" says Harry.
"No, no, no! You **are**
a lovely locust."

The trouble is, as I've found out, you really **CANNOT FOCUS**!

"I focus when I drive," she says. "It's too important not to."

Harry nods. "When on the road, you've absolutely got to!"

It's Lola's first day on the bus. Her confidence is growing.

Stop one...

Stop two...

They chug along.
But then...

Lola's seen a different road. "Ooh, this way does look fun!"

She takes the road and stares ahead, forgetting everyone.

All at once, she stops and shouts. "I'm driving THE WRONG WAY!"

"Those bugs still waiting for my bus... Oh dear, what will they say?"

BUMBLE'S BIG CIRCUS!

They say a lot.

Lola sobs. She's lost
THREE jobs.

Don't cry, there!
My name's Fran.

"I was on the bus with you, and I have got a plan..."

Soon Lola has a
big, green bus.

Four beetles climb on board the bus.

They see the sea and eat ice cream.

Now Lola has a job she loves. She focuses all day.

And crowds of eager
bugs line up, to ride
the Lola way.

Designed by Laura Nelson Norris
Edited by Jenny Tyler

Reading consultant: Alison Kelly
With thanks to Holly Docherty,
Special Educational Needs Co-ordinator (SENCo)

First published in 2024 by Usborne Publishing Limited,
83-85 Saffron Hill, London EC1N 8RT, United Kingdom. usborne.com

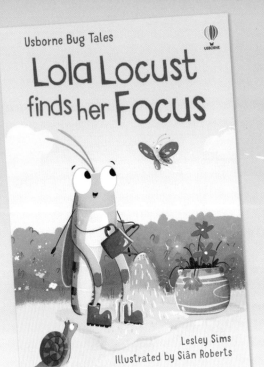

Usborne Bug Tales

Lola Locust
finds her Focus

Lesley Sims
Illustrated by Siân Roberts

Each book is
a fun surprise.

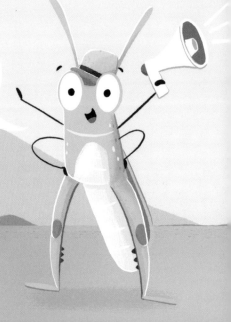